STRAIGHT FROM THE BEAR'S MOUTH

STRAIGHT

FROM THE

BEAR'S MOUTH

THE STORY OF PHOTOSYNTHESIS

WRITTEN AND ILLUSTRATED BY

BILL ROSS

Atheneum Books for Young Readers

Simon & Schuster

New York

Atheneum Books for Young Readers
An Imprint of Simon & Schuster Children's Publishing
Division
1230 Avenue of the Americas
New York, New York 10020
Text copyright © 1995 by Bill Ross
Book design by Trish Parcell Watts
The text of this book is set in 11/13 Garamond Light.
Printed in U.S.A.
Library of Congress Catalog Card Number: 95–60387
10 9 8 7 6 5 4 3 2 1

For my parents

WHAT ON EARTH DO
THOSE LITTLE SEEDS EAT?

Aspen trees grow from tiny seeds that look like fuzzy specks blowing in the wind in the spring and early summer. Dina and Jake had never paid much attention to these fuzzy seeds before. But now they were taking a science camp during their summer break, and they needed a good project. So they caught some of the aspen seeds that floated by, to have a closer look.

How could such tiny seeds produce trees that tower over 50 feet in the air? Their biology teacher, Dr. Mildew, helped them find out. Not only was Dr. Mildew clever, but he was also pretty weird. He had a number of unusual hobbies, including wrestling his pet bear at public events. But for this aspen project, his experiments were so strange that his past deeds seemed almost normal. But the results of the experiments were astounding!

Although people tended to snicker at the funny ways of Dr. M, as they called him, he was really the most respected scientist in town. Dr. M says that the most important step in becoming a good scientist is to ask good questions in a clear manner.

He suggested three steps for forming and answering proper questions:

1. It is important to ask the *right* question. Usually you have to poke around in your subject a while before you know what question to ask. The question is actually expressed as a statement called a *hypothesis*. For example, instead of asking: "Do aspen trees eat soil and drink water to grow into big trees?" you state a hypothesis. The hypothesis might be: "Aspen trees eat soil and drink water to grow into big trees."

2. The next step is to test the hypothesis with experiments to see if it is true or false. Every test of your hypothesis is a *treatment*. And each treatment must be accompanied by a *control*. For example, in order to test if aspen trees need water to grow, your treatment would be to withhold water from a group of aspen trees. Your control would be to provide a similar group of trees with water. All other conditions would be identical for both the treatments and the controls.

3. Finally, the results of the experiment are recorded, and the hypothesis is determined to be true or false. During this step, scientists read about experiments that other scientists have done earlier in order to help explain the results of their own experiments.

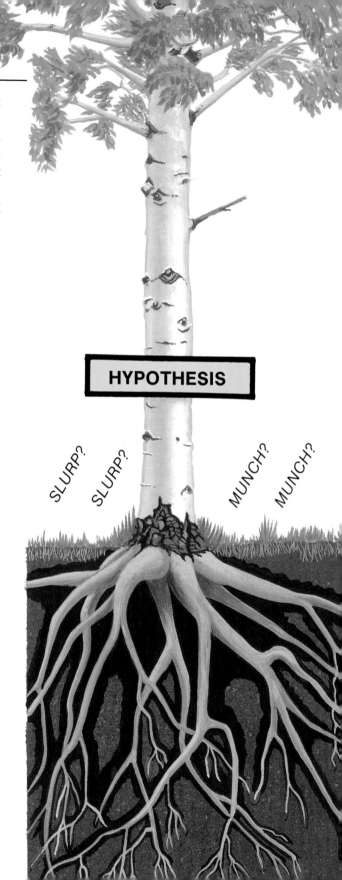

HYPOTHESIS

SLURP? SLURP? MUNCH? MUNCH?

Dina and Jake knew that tiny aspen seeds, which look a lot like fuzzy dandelion seeds, would have to eat a whole bunch of something in order to produce trees 50 feet tall. Since trees grow out of the *soil* and seem to need *water,* they thought their hypothesis should be: *Aspen seeds eat soil and drink water to produce big trees.*

If trees eat mainly soil to grow so big, then big holes would have to appear under large trees where they have been eating. Dina quickly volunteered to take notes as she handed Jake the shovel. He dug down under a big aspen tree, but no large holes were found in the soil. Dina recorded, "If aspen trees eat soil at all, they must not eat much of it."

Next they noticed clumps of fuzzy seeds stuck in the mud along a little creek bed. Wherever the seeds were in wet soil, they germinated and had produced little green seedlings. But away from the creek, on dry soil, not a seed had sprouted. So Dina recorded, "Aspen trees do need water in order to grow."

These observations seemed to indicate that the hypothesis was only half right. This left Dina and Jake with a very puzzling problem. Certainly trees were made from more than just water. But, if trees didn't eat much soil, and just drank water, where did they get all that other stuff that trees are made of? Certainly trees don't grow right out of thin air—or do they?

DR. MILDEW'S STRANGE EXPERIMENTS

Dina and Jake decided to ask Dr. M for his advice on choosing a hypothesis, since their first try didn't work out very well. As usual, Dr. M's advice seemed pretty weird. But, weird or not, Dr. M had the kind of reputation that was not to be ignored. Dr. M spent part of his summer wrestling his bear at county fairs. His partner in this enterprise was a big brown bear named Burpy who lived in a cage in his backyard. Dr. M and Burpy went on the road with their wrestling act every other week. The neighbors claimed that the two gladiators often dined together on heaping tubs of potato salad at the picnic table in Dr. M's backyard.

When Dina and Jake approached Dr. M

with their hypothesis, he told them to dig up 12 little aspen seedlings of equal size. They were to put each of the 12 seedlings into a separate clay pot so that they could be moved about as required by the experiments. Then he took Dina and Jake to inspect Burpy Bear's living quarters.

Burpy's cage was about 20 feet square. But the big bear was especially fond of sprawling out in one particular corner of the cage and snoozing after he'd porked out on a bushel or so of potato salad. Jake noted that grass grew all around the outside edge of Burpy's cage, but it was particularly robust near his favorite sleeping corner. They wondered aloud why that was, but Dr. M only smiled.

TWO CONTROLS AND TWO TREATMENTS

IN DARKNESS	IN SUNLIGHT

When Dr. M and Burpy are out of town (Controls)

When Burpy is home (Treatment)

Each potted tree was identified with a number. Three trees were to be placed near Burpy's favorite corner only at night, when it was *dark*. Then they were to be removed 100 feet away from the cage to grow with the other plants for the rest of the day.

A different set of three trees was to be placed near Burpy's corner only during *daylight*.

The *control* plants were to be put in place near Burpy's cage every day during the week Burpy and Dr. M were *out of town* with their wrestling act.

The set of *treatment* plants was to be put in place every day for the week Burpy was *home*. So the only difference between the controls and the treatments was the presence or absence of the bear.

Dina and Jake knew better than to ask why; they just did it.

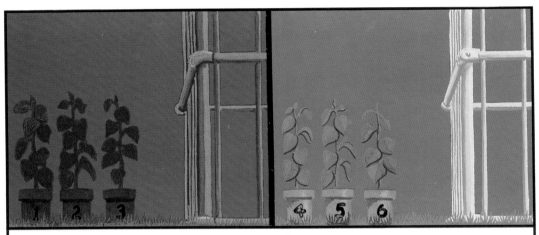

Controls

When the bear was gone, all 12 trees grew the same amount. The control trees (trees 1 through 6) continued to grow at the same rate during the second week when they remained 100 feet away from Burpy's cage, both day and night.

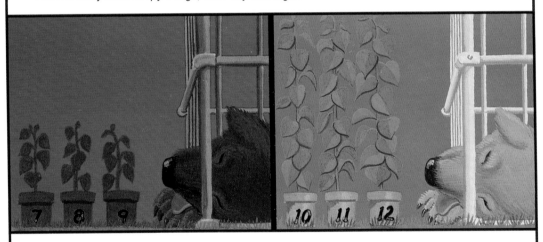

Treatments

Trees 7, 8, and 9 grew the same as the controls while Burpy was gone. But their growth was retarded when they spent their nights in the presence of the bear.

Trees 10, 11, and 12 grew the same as the controls during the first week, but grew twice as fast as the controls in the sunlight when Burpy was home.

The first week was really boring for Dina and Jake, because Burpy was out of town. They took turns with night duty and day duty, but none of their careful work seemed to make any difference—at the end of the week, all of the 12 plants looked alike.

But the second week—with Burpy home again—was something else! Placing the aspen plants near Burpy's favorite corner when he was home was pretty spooky. Even though he spent most of his time sleeping, he usually stuck his snoozing snout through the bars in his cage close to where the kids put the plants. Dina and Jake could often see his big fangs. And the breath of this snoring bear wasn't all that great either—Dr. M never spared the onions when he made his famous potato salad.

As the week progressed, Dina and Jake couldn't believe what they saw. The three plants that had night duty with Burpy were much smaller than the controls. But the plants placed near Burpy in the sunlight grew like mad. They were twice the size of the control plants that had been put out in Burpy's absence.

The evidence was overwhelming. Aspen seedlings eat *bear breath* in order to grow into big trees!

But the data also presented some troubling questions. Why do plants still grow where there are no bears? And why did the same bear breath that caused the aspen trees to grow like mad in the *sunlight* cause them to be stunted at night, in the *dark*?

Pretty dumb experiments, right?

Wrong! The observations that bear breath retards the growth of trees in the dark, but causes them to grow like mad in the sunlight are experimental results of great scientific importance.

DR. MILDEW'S CLUES TO THE MYSTERY

Results from scientific experiments are not always easy to explain. Many times scientists have to search in libraries to see if their results can be explained by previous experiments of other scientists. Dr. M knew a lot about recorded science. Although he rarely answered entire questions for his students, he did provide them with clues to their mysteries. He presented Dina and Jake with seven important clues that allowed them to explain their new hypothesis: *Bear breath retards the growth of seedlings in the dark, but causes them to grow like mad in sunlight.*

In order to know how plants grow, you must know what they are made of. All things are made up of tiny, invisible building blocks called *atoms*. Ninety different kinds of atoms occur naturally in the earth's crust. Each different kind of atom is called a *chemical element,* such as the elements iron, copper, and carbon, to name just a few.

Two different kinds of substances exist:

1. Substances produced by living organisms—such as leaves, fur, and skin—are called *organic matter.*

2. Substances not produced by living organisms—such as rocks and metals—are called *inorganic minerals.*

These are not very exact terms, because much organic matter also contains minerals. But these are useful terms if we apply them in a general way.

The neat thing about organic matter is that it is easy to learn about, because most organic matter consists mainly of only three different elements: *carbon, hydrogen,* and *oxygen.* The chemical symbol for carbon is C, the symbol for hydrogen is H, and the symbol for oxygen is O. All living creatures must also contain several

different *minerals.* But minerals are present in organic tissues in much smaller amounts than carbon (C), hydrogen (H), and oxygen (O).

ORGANIC MATTER CONSISTS MAINLY OF ONLY 3 CHEMICAL ELEMENTS.

ELEMENT	SYMBOL
Carbon	C
Hydrogen	H
Oxygen	O

PLANTS ALSO REQUIRE SEVERAL *MINERALS* IN ORDER TO GROW.

Nitrogen	N
Potassium	K
Calcium	Ca
Phosphorus	P
Magnesium	Mg
Iron	Fe
Sulfur	S
Chlorine	Cl
Copper	Cu
Manganese	Mn
Zinc	Zn
Molybdenum	Mo
Boron	B

(SOME PLANTS ALSO REQUIRE)

Cobalt	Co
Sodium	Na

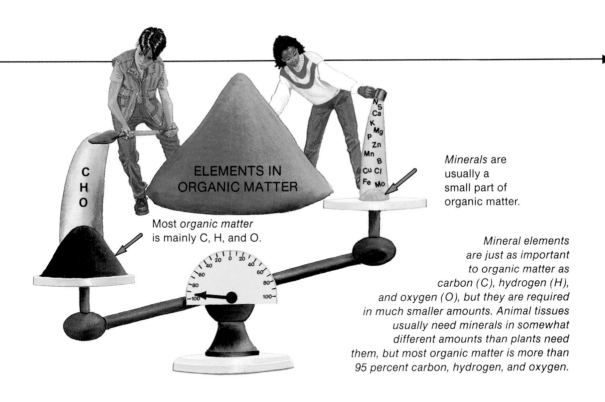

ELEMENTS IN ORGANIC MATTER

C H O

Most *organic matter* is mainly C, H, and O.

Minerals are usually a small part of organic matter.

Mineral elements are just as important to organic matter as carbon (C), hydrogen (H), and oxygen (O), but they are required in much smaller amounts. Animal tissues usually need minerals in somewhat different amounts than plants need them, but most organic matter is more than 95 percent carbon, hydrogen, and oxygen.

When wood burns completely, more than 99 percent of it turns into smoke. This smoke consists of gases that are made up mainly of the elements carbon (C), hydrogen (H), and oxygen (O). The 1 percent substance that remains behind as ash consists mainly of mineral elements in wood, such as iron, copper, calcium, and the many others listed earlier.

When 100 pounds of wood burn completely, more than 99 pounds become gases composed mainly of C, H, and O.

Less than one pound of burned wood remains behind as ashes.

Dead creatures just disappear into thin air.

Why aren't big piles of dead plants and animals lying all around? Where do plants and animals go when they die?

Oh sure, when plants and animals die, bugs and worms and microbes all eat the remains. But all of these creatures, including their droppings, never end up weighing as much as the dead stuff they eat. Where does the missing organic matter go?

Burning wood turns into invisible gases.

Watching wood burn gives us a hint about where organic matter goes when it disappears. If wood burns completely, most of it will disappear into the air mainly as two invisible gases. These gases are *carbon dioxide* (CO_2) and *water* (H_2O) vapor (steam). Notice that these gases contain only carbon (C), hydrogen (H), and oxygen (O).

But you don't start a fire to produce CO_2 and H_2O. Usually you want the *heat energy* that is released from the burning wood. Energy is an invisible force that causes *work* or *motion* to happen (see page 18). During combustion (fire) the carbon and hydrogen atoms from wood molecules combine with oxygen from the air to form carbon dioxide and water. As CO_2 and H_2O form, energy is released (see page 21). This energy causes these gas molecules, along with air molecules, to move and vibrate rapidly. Rapidly moving and vibrating molecules produce *heat.*

As creatures die, their bodies are converted into invisible gases by the organisms that eat and decay them.

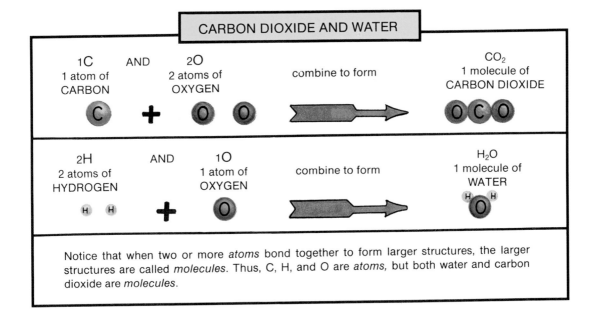

CARBON DIOXIDE AND WATER

1C 1 atom of CARBON	AND	2O 2 atoms of OXYGEN	combine to form	CO_2 1 molecule of CARBON DIOXIDE

2H 2 atoms of HYDROGEN	AND	1O 1 atom of OXYGEN	combine to form	H_2O 1 molecule of WATER

Notice that when two or more *atoms* bond together to form larger structures, the larger structures are called *molecules*. Thus, C, H, and O are *atoms*, but both water and carbon dioxide are *molecules*.

Living creatures use only part of the food they eat to form visible body *structures*. Most food is eaten to get the *chemical energy* that is stored in the organic molecules that make up food.

The body cells of animals release energy (called *chemical energy*) from organic molecules by using a process similar to combustion (see pages 20–23). This energy-releasing process converts the organic molecules in food into, guess what? The food is converted into the same two gases that are produced by fire: CO_2 and H_2O vapor. So animal breath and smoke from fires are similar.

As mentioned earlier, *energy* is an invisible force that causes *movement* or *work* to be done. Water in a high mountain lake has energy (called potential energy) for gouging out streambeds and turning waterwheels as it is pulled downhill by gravity. Energy occurs in several forms, such as *mechanical, electrical, light, heat,* and *chemical.* Chemical bonds contain *chemical energy.*

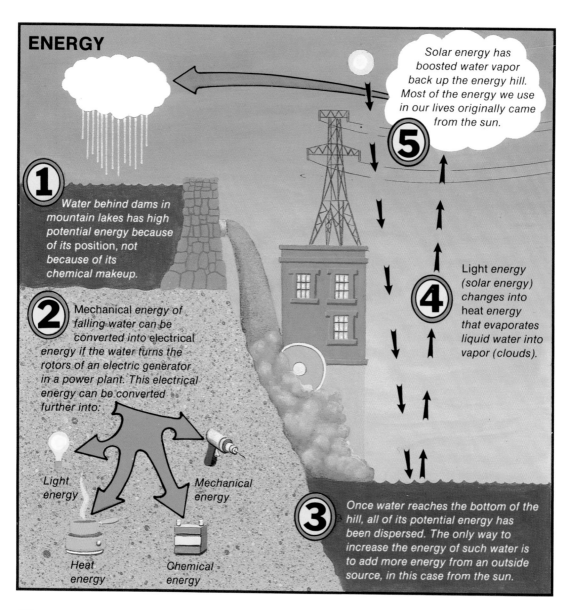

ENERGY

1 Water behind dams in mountain lakes has high potential energy because of its position, *not because of its chemical makeup.*

2 Mechanical energy of falling water can be converted into electrical energy if the water turns the rotors of an electric generator in a power plant. This electrical energy can be converted further into:

Light energy

Mechanical energy

Heat energy

Chemical energy

3 Once water reaches the bottom of the hill, all of its potential energy has been dispersed. The only way to increase the energy of such water is to add more energy from an outside source, in this case from the sun.

4 Light *energy* (solar energy) changes into heat energy that evaporates liquid water into vapor (clouds).

5 Solar energy has boosted water vapor back up the energy hill. Most of the energy we use in our lives originally came from the sun.

CHEMICAL BONDS

The force that causes two atoms to stick together in a molecule is a chemical bond. Each kind of atom can form a specific number of total bonds with other atoms. Carbon can form four bonds, oxygen two bonds, and hydrogen one bond. When a carbon atom (C) bonds to a hydrogen atom (H), the bond is called a C–H bond. Oxygen (O) bonds to hydrogen (H) to form an O–H bond, carbon bonds to oxygen to form a C–O bond, and carbon bonds to other carbon atoms to form C–C bonds.

Structural Formula	Chemical Formula
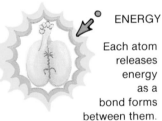 Ethane (Found in Natural Gas) C–C bond C–H bond	C_2H_6
Carbon Dioxide C–O bond	CO_2
O–H bond Water	H_2O

Energy is *released* as bonds *form*.

ENERGY

Two free, high-energy atoms are attracted to each other.

ENERGY

Each atom releases energy as a bond forms between them.

Dispersing bond energy

Atoms within molecules have less energy than free, unbonded atoms.

Every atom carries chemical energy with it. Free, unbonded atoms carry their maximum amount of energy—they are at the top of their energy hill. Each time a bond forms, a part of the atom's energy is released, making the bond stable. This is like two nervous people releasing nervous energy to become more stable as they hold hands. A different amount of energy is released as each kind of bond forms. Chemical energy can be released from fires as heat, or it can be released as mechanical energy to move muscles in animals.

As bonds *break*, energy is *absorbed*.

CHEMICAL BOND

Atoms in the molecule have low energy with a strong bond between them.

The bond becomes less stable as energy is absorbed.

As the bond breaks, each atom carries the absorbed energy with it.

In order to break a bond, the same amount of energy that was released when the bond formed, must be absorbed back by the bond. This absorbed energy causes the atoms to come apart. The atoms that separate at a breaking bond carry this absorbed energy with them. Thus, energy is released when bonds form, and energy is absorbed when bonds break.

4 CLUE
ENERGY IS RELEASED FROM ORGANIC MATTER AS CO₂ AND H₂O ARE FORMED.

What is so important about the carbon dioxide and water in both smoke from fires and in animal breath? In both cases, the CO_2 and H_2O are produced when *energy* is *released* from organic mole- cules. Energy is released as fires produce smoke. And energy is released as working animals produce CO_2 and H_2O in their breath.

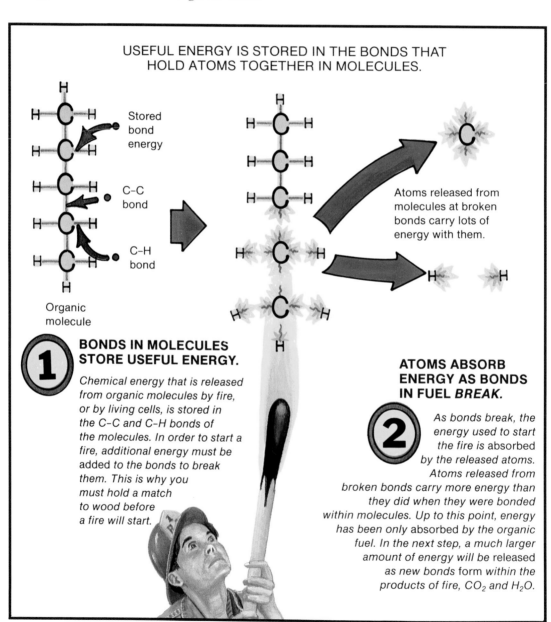

USEFUL ENERGY IS STORED IN THE BONDS THAT HOLD ATOMS TOGETHER IN MOLECULES.

Stored bond energy

C–C bond

C–H bond

Organic molecule

Atoms released from molecules at broken bonds carry lots of energy with them.

1 BONDS IN MOLECULES STORE USEFUL ENERGY.

Chemical energy that is released from organic molecules by fire, or by living cells, is stored in the C–C and C–H bonds of the molecules. In order to start a fire, additional energy must be added to the bonds to break them. This is why you must hold a match to wood before a fire will start.

ATOMS ABSORB ENERGY AS BONDS IN FUEL BREAK.

2

As bonds break, the energy used to start the fire is absorbed by the released atoms. Atoms released from broken bonds carry more energy than they did when they were bonded within molecules. Up to this point, energy has been only absorbed by the organic fuel. In the next step, a much larger amount of energy will be released as new bonds form within the products of fire, CO₂ and H₂O.

3 OXYGEN IS A VERY SPECIAL ATOM.

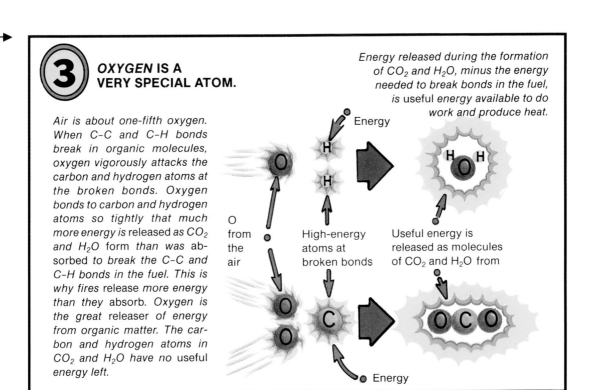

Air is about one-fifth oxygen. When C–C and C–H bonds break in organic molecules, oxygen vigorously attacks the carbon and hydrogen atoms at the broken bonds. Oxygen bonds to carbon and hydrogen atoms so tightly that much more energy is released as CO_2 and H_2O form than was absorbed to break the C–C and C–H bonds in the fuel. This is why fires release more energy than they absorb. Oxygen is the great releaser of energy from organic matter. The carbon and hydrogen atoms in CO_2 and H_2O have no useful energy left.

Energy released during the formation of CO_2 and H_2O, minus the energy needed to break bonds in the fuel, is useful energy available to do work and produce heat.

Energy

O from the air

High-energy atoms at broken bonds

Useful energy is released as molecules of CO_2 and H_2O from

Energy

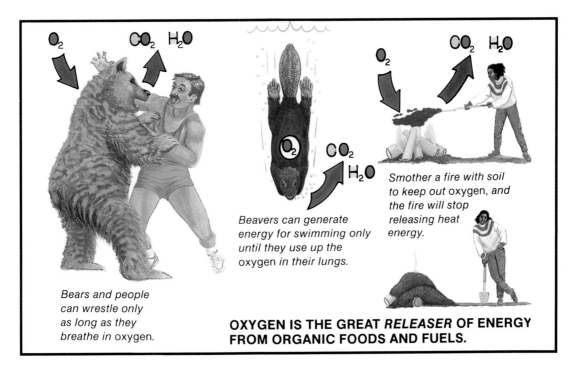

Bears and people can wrestle only as long as they breathe in oxygen.

Beavers can generate energy for swimming only until they use up the oxygen in their lungs.

Smother a fire with soil to keep out oxygen, and the fire will stop releasing heat energy.

OXYGEN IS THE GREAT *RELEASER* OF ENERGY FROM ORGANIC FOODS AND FUELS.

An *aerobic* process is one that requires *oxygen*. Fire is an aerobic process, because it adds oxygen to organic matter to form carbon dioxide and water. Fat bears don't have fires burning in them, but the cells of bears use similar chemical reactions to release energy from the organic molecules in food as fires use to release heat energy from organic molecules in fuels. Living cells, though, are able to break C–C and C–H bonds at body temperatures.

And when cells add oxygen to carbon and hydrogen atoms to produce CO_2 and H_2O, most of the *energy* that is released is used to do *work* in living cells rather than to produce *heat*. That is why cells don't burn up from heat energy. The process of "burning" (or adding oxygen to) foods inside living cells to generate energy is called *aerobic respiration*.

Fat bears pant during *aerobic* exercise, such as wrestling, in order to bring lots of

In with the good air
O_2

oxygen into their lungs. The oxygen travels in their blood to their muscle cells, where it bonds with hydrogen atoms from bear fat to form water during the bear's *aerobic respiration*. At the same time, additional oxygen from water (H_2O) forms bonds with carbon atoms in bear fat to form carbon dioxide (CO_2). The *energy* released during the formation of this CO_2 and H_2O is used to make the bears' muscles move. The CO_2 is of no further use to the bears because it has no more useful energy left in it. So the CO_2 is removed from the bear as bear breath.

If an animal were confined to a small, airtight container, all of the oxygen in the container soon would be converted to CO_2 and H_2O. Without a supply of oxygen, the animal would be unable to generate enough energy to stay alive; it would suffocate in CO_2.

Out with the bad air
CO_2 and H_2O

Plants absorb CO_2 in order to make new organic matter.

Plants *release* CO_2 as they break down organic matter during respiration.

Plants

Plants release CO_2 during respiration, but they absorb much more of it than they release during a process called photosynthesis. Over time, plants absorb much more CO_2 than they release.

Animals

Animals cannot absorb CO_2 out of the air and make organic matter from it. They must get all of their carbon and energy from plant tissues or from tissues of animals that have eaten plants.

Energy is trapped and stored.

Energy is lost as heat.

SUN

Green plants may trap and store solar energy, but animals cannot. Plants then use their stored energy to build new organic matter.

In order to make new organic matter from burned-out carbon (CO_2) and burned-out hydrogen (H_2O), the oxygen (O) atoms must be broken away from CO_2 and H_2O. The broken C–O and O–H bonds are then replaced with energy-rich C–C and C–H bonds to form new organic molecules. This reverses the processes of respiration and combustion. *Energy* is required to break the C–O and O–H bonds of the CO_2 and H_2O.

Plants are green because they contain a green pigment called *chlorophyll*. This pigment can capture *energy* from sunlight. H atoms are charged with solar energy as they are ripped away from H_2O. Energy from charged-up H is then used to remove O from C–O bonds and to direct the formation of C–C and C–H bonds in organic matter. Only part of the energy absorbed to break C–O and O–H bonds is released when new C–C and C–H bonds form, so these new bonds retain solar energy.

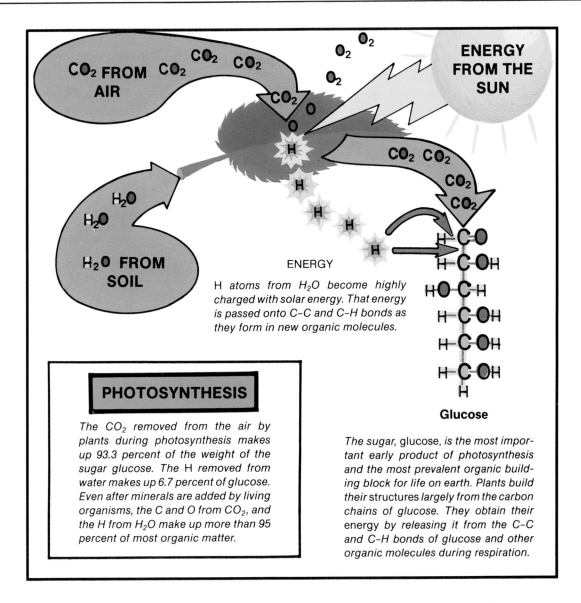

ENERGY FROM THE SUN

CO₂ FROM AIR

H₂O FROM SOIL

ENERGY

H atoms from H_2O become highly charged with solar energy. That energy is passed onto C–C and C–H bonds as they form in new organic molecules.

Glucose

PHOTOSYNTHESIS

The CO_2 removed from the air by plants during photosynthesis makes up 93.3 percent of the weight of the sugar glucose. The H removed from water makes up 6.7 percent of glucose. Even after minerals are added by living organisms, the C and O from CO_2, and the H from H_2O make up more than 95 percent of most organic matter.

The sugar, glucose, is the most important early product of photosynthesis and the most prevalent organic building block for life on earth. Plants build their structures largely from the carbon chains of glucose. They obtain their energy by releasing it from the C–C and C–H bonds of glucose and other organic molecules during respiration.

The word *photo* means light, and *synthesis* means to make something. So the process of making new *organic matter* from *inorganic* CO_2 and H_2O using *solar energy* (sunlight) is called *photosynthesis*.

The energy added to organic molecules during *photosynthesis* is the same energy that comes back out of organic matter during *aerobic respiration* in living cells or when organic fuels are *burned*. The energy in our organic foods is used to keep our bodies alive and warm. Energy from our organic fuels, such as coal, oil, and wood, runs our machines and heats our buildings.

Most (but not all) living organisms constantly take oxygen out of the air to support their aerobic respiration. So why doesn't air run out of oxygen?

As photosynthesis takes place within plants, solar energy is added to water in order to break the hydrogen atoms (the H_2 part) away from H_2O. The O part of H_2O is then released into the air. Actually, released atoms of O combine, two at a

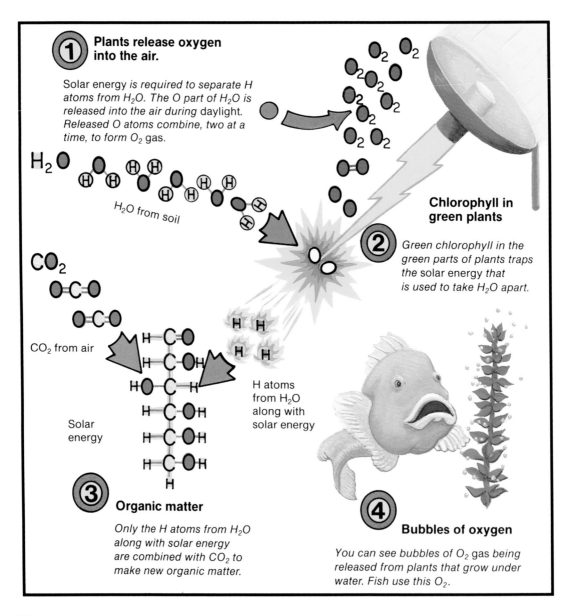

① Plants release oxygen into the air.

Solar energy *is required to separate H atoms from H_2O. The O part of H_2O is released into the air during daylight. Released O atoms combine, two at a time, to form O_2 gas.*

H_2O from soil

CO_2 from air

Solar energy

③ Organic matter

Only the H atoms from H_2O along with solar energy are combined with CO_2 to make new organic matter.

Chlorophyll in green plants

② *Green chlorophyll in the green parts of plants traps the solar energy that is used to take H_2O apart.*

H atoms from H_2O along with solar energy

④ Bubbles of oxygen

You can see bubbles of O_2 gas being released from plants that grow under water. Fish use this O_2.

time, to form *molecules of oxygen gas* (O_2). Remember, plants require *solar energy* to remove H_2 from H_2O. Thus, photosynthesis cannot occur in the *dark*.

Plants, just like you, must constantly *absorb* O_2 for their *aerobic respiration*. So, in the dark, plants only *absorb* O_2 and *release* CO_2. But in the light, plants also *absorb* CO_2 and *release* O_2 during photosynthesis. Over long periods, plants release much more O_2 than they absorb, and they absorb much more CO_2 than they release. Most of the O_2 now in the air was released by plants during photosynthesis.

Why Did Bear Breath Retard Seedlings Growth in the Dark?

After Burpy Bear filled his belly with Dr. M's scrumptious potato salad, he had plenty of organic fuel for rebuilding his exhausted body after hard sessions of wrestling practice. His aerobic respiration roared away, filling his breath with CO_2 and H_2O vapor. The little seedlings were smothered with the bear breath that poured from Burpy's snout as the bear snored away the night. The trees desperately needed *oxygen* for their own *aerobic respiration,* but all they could get from the air was the worthless CO_2 in Burpy's breath. Much of the organic matter produced in green leaves during the day moves to other plant tissues to support growth during the night. But such growth requires respiration. Without oxygen, night growth could not occur, so seedling growth was retarded.

Why Did the Same Bear Breath Cause the Seedlings to Grow Fast in Sunlight?

In sunlight, plants produce all the O_2 they need as they break H atoms away from H_2O. And with lots of oxygen to run their *aerobic respiration,* the seedlings were able to absorb the extra CO_2 that billowed from Burpy's snout, whether he was practicing his wrestling or just snoring in his corner, and use it in their *photosynthesis.* Bear breath could really speed up photosynthesis, because the normally low levels of CO_2 in air can limit the normal rate of photosynthesis. The plants were able to use the new organic matter from their faster rate of photosynthesis to make new roots and leaves and other stuff that seedlings are made of. Some commercial growers add CO_2 to their greenhouses to increase the rate of plant growth.

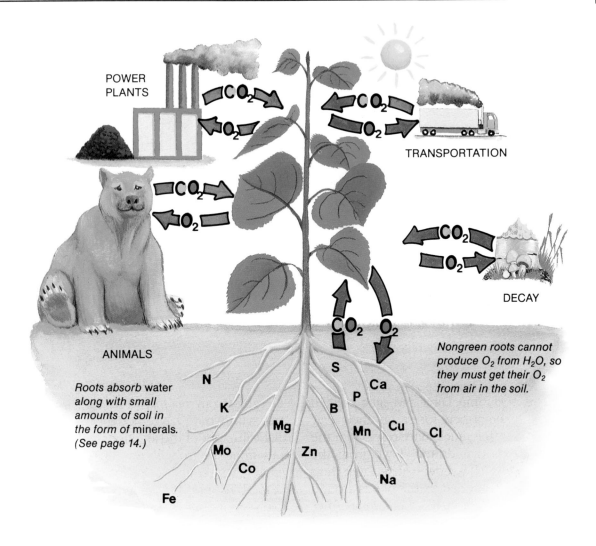

POWER PLANTS

CO_2

O_2

CO_2

O_2

TRANSPORTATION

CO_2

O_2

CO_2

O_2

DECAY

CO_2 O_2

ANIMALS

Roots absorb water along with small amounts of soil in the form of minerals. (See page 14.)

Nongreen roots cannot produce O_2 from H_2O, so they must get their O_2 from air in the soil.

N

K

S

Ca

P

B

Mg

Mn

Cu

Cl

Mo

Zn

Co

Na

Fe

And so the answer became clear. The tiny seedlings did absorb a small amount of soil through their roots in order to get minerals such as nitrogen, phosphorus, potassium, iron, zinc, and many others. But more than 95 pounds out of each 100 pounds of the dry substance of trees is made only of *carbon, hydrogen,* and *oxygen.* The C and O come from CO_2 in the air. The H comes from H_2O in the soil. The *energy* that puts new organic matter together comes from the sunlight that plants capture and use in their *photosynthesis.* Then, when the little seedlings needed energy to build new leaves, stems, and roots, they released that energy from the organic food that they made from scratch. They released the energy by adding O_2 to that food using *aerobic respiration.* So that's what little seeds eat to grow into large trees.

The next time Dina and Jake walked through the aspen forest on their way home, they felt much more respect for the fuzzy seeds that drifted down from the trees above. They now realized that their very lives depended on the plants around them. The plants gave them their *food*, their *shelter*, and their *oxygen*. Even their *clothes*, which came from cotton fibers, or from petroleum in the case of polyesters, all came from *photosynthetic* organisms. And who would have thought that all of that came out of the air, along with water and minerals from the soil? Then *solar energy*, which also came out of the air, helped to put the organic molecules together and to give living creatures the *chemical energy* they need to stay alive.

Awesome!

All pronunciations were taken from P. H. Raven et al., *Biology of Plants,* 2nd ed., Worth Publishers, Inc., New York, 1976, or from *The Random House College Dictionary,* rev. ed., 1980.

AEROBIC (āˊĕr ōˊ bĭk) Aerobic organisms require free oxygen for life. They generate energy by combining the hydrogen in organic matter with oxygen to form H_2O.

ANAEROBIC (ăn ā ĕr ōˊ bik) Anaerobic organisms can live without oxygen. Some organisms are actually poisoned by oxygen and cannot live in its presence.

ATOM (ătˊ ŭm) An atom is the smallest piece of a chemical element that has all the properties of that element. Atoms are the building blocks for molecules.

BOND Atoms are attracted to each other, and this attraction causes them to stick together. A bond is the point where atoms attach to each other. Energy is released when bonds form. Energy must be absorbed by atoms before bonds between them will break. Solar energy is absorbed by H atoms as they break away from H_2O. That same amount of energy is released as bonds form within molecules of H_2O.

CHEMICAL ENERGY Energy that is associated with the chemical bonds between the atoms of molecules.

CHLOROPHYLL (klōˊro fĭl) Chlorophyll is the green pigment in plants. Pigments are substances that are colored because they absorb some colors of light while reflecting other colors. White sunlight is made up of all of the colors in a rainbow. Chlorophyll traps the energy in blue and red light, but reflects green light. Leaves are green, because the green part of sunlight reflects from them.

ENERGY Energy is a force that causes motion or work to be done. Energy has several forms, such as heat, light, mechanical, electrical, and chemical. Energy stored in chemical bonds is called chemical energy.

MINERALS Minerals are atoms or molecules that are produced by forces other than living cells. They often do not contain C, H, or O. Iron oxide (rust) and sodium chloride (table salt) are examples of inorganic minerals.

MOLECULE (mŏlˊe kūl) When two or more atoms bond together, the group of bonded atoms is a molecule. Molecules that contain more than one type of element are also called compounds. H_2O is a molecule of water made up of atoms of H and O.

ORGANIC (ôr ganˊ ik) Substances that are produced by living organisms and contain carbon, hydrogen, and often oxygen.

ORGANIC MATTER A general term used to describe any collection of organic molecules. It usually refers to tissues of organisms, dead or alive.

OXIDATION (ŏkˊsĭ dāˊshən) The process of adding oxygen to a molecule. Oxidation causes the loss of energy from molecules. Both fire and respiration are oxidation reactions that release energy from organic matter.

PHOTOSYNTHESIS (fōˊtō sĭnˊthe sĭs) The process of converting light energy into chemical energy in order to make organic molecules from CO_2 and H_2O.

PIGMENT A substance that absorbs some colors of light while reflecting others. The color of the pigment is produced by the colors of light that the pigment reflects.

RESPIRATION (resˊpə rāˊshən) The process whereby organic molecules are combined with oxygen inside living cells to release energy, CO_2 and H_2O.

SEED Seeds contain a tiny, developing plant (called an embryo) inside them. Also, most seeds contain stored food that feeds the developing embryo until it becomes a big enough seedling to support itself with photosynthesis.

INDEX

GAYLORD